STIRRING UP TROUBLE

A Warlocks MacGregor Novella

MICHELLE M. PILLOW

Michelle M. Pillow® - MichellePillow.com

Stirring Up Trouble (*Warlocks MacGregor*®) © copyright 2015 -
2018 by Michelle M. Pillow

First Electronic Printing Dec 2015

Cover art © Copyright 2015

Edited by Heidi Moore

Published by The Raven Books LLC

ISBN-13: 978-1-62501-166-4

About Stirring Up Trouble

Magick, Mischief and Kilts.
Some Warlocks excel at brewing up trouble.

When Scottish Warlock Fergus MacGregor is around their new neighbor Donna Montgomery, he feels something he hasn't felt for a long time. He is still holding on to the memory of his first love who died centuries ago. He's tried everything to bring Elspeth back from the dead. None of his magic spells, potions, sorcery or incantations have worked. His family thinks it's time he moves on.

Is fate giving him a second chance at love, or will falling for Donna stir a powerful supernatural force that intends to cause nothing but trouble?

A *Warlocks MacGregor*® Novella

Warlocks MacGregor® Series

SCOTTISH MAGICKAL WARLOCKS

Love Potions
Spellbound
Stirring Up Trouble
Cauldrons and Confessions
Spirits and Spells
Kisses and Curses
Magick and Mischief
A Dash of Destiny
Night Magick
More Coming Soon

Visit www.MichellePillow.com for details.

Author Updates

To stay informed about when a new book is released sign up for updates:

http://michellepillow.com/author-updates/

Michelle's Bestselling Series

SHAPE-SHIFTER ROMANCES

Dragon Lords Series

Barbarian Prince
Perfect Prince
Dark Prince
Warrior Prince
His Highness The Duke
The Stubborn Lord
The Reluctant Lord
The Impatient Lord
The Dragon's Queen

Lords of the Var® Series

The Savage King
The Playful Prince
The Bound Prince
The Rogue Prince
The Pirate Prince

Captured by a Dragon-Shifter Series

Determined Prince
Rebellious Prince
Stranded with the Cajun
Hunted by the Dragon
Mischievous Prince
Headstrong Prince

Space Lords Series

His Frost Maiden
His Fire Maiden
His Metal Maiden
His Earth Maiden
His Woodland Maiden

Having trouble finding the books?
Vendors links sometimes change.
Updated Buy Links Here

To learn more about the Dragon Lords World
series of books and to stay up to date on the latest
book list visit www.MichellePillow.com

To B. I hope you find magick in the world.

Note from the Author

People know magic is fake—card tricks and illusions, magicians and entertainers. But there is an older magick, a powerful force hidden from modern eyes, buried in folklore and myths, remembered by the few who practice the old ways and respect the lessons of past generations.

The term "warlock" is a variation on the Old English word *waerloga*, primarily used by the Scots. It meant traitor, monster or deceiver. The MacGregor Clan does not agree with how history has labeled their kind. To them, warlock means magick, family and immortality. This book is not meant to be a portrayal of modern-day witches or those who have such beliefs. The MacGregors are a magickal class all their own.

As with all my books, this is pure fantasy. In real life, please always practice safe sex and magic.

Author recommends reading series in order of release for the simple fact it's more fun that way, though each book can be read as a standalone if you prefer.

Chapter One

PROLOGUE

Winter, 1591, England-Scotland Border

"Do not leave me." The pain was unbearable in that moment of waiting, of knowing the end was near, knowing these were the last seconds he would have with his Elspeth. Tears streamed down his love's face as he reached for her in the snow. This was not how their life together was supposed to go. They were supposed to be immortal. They were supposed to have each other forever.

All of Fergus MacGregor's warlock powers could not make time last. That didn't mean he didn't try. He cast every spell he knew, and even some he didn't. He willed time to stop, and for a short while, it stalled.

The trickle of blood streaming along her pale cheek slowed until it barely traveled over her flesh.

Her eyes shone with pain. To keep her in this state was too cruel. She was locked in agony. There was no spell he knew of that could transfer her death into him. Yet he tried to do that too.

"I'm coming with ya, my heart," Fergus said, more like a plea. He let his powers slip from her, unable to prolong her suffering any longer. He felt around for his sword only to discover he'd dropped it several feet away. He reached his hand out, using his magick to call it to him. The blade began to slide in the snow only to stop when his wife's voice interrupted his action.

"Malina," Elspeth whispered, making him think of their niece. The baby was silent, her cry bound with a spell. "Protect."

How could he deny the desperate need in her gaze? Fergus nodded. "Aye."

"Whatever is beyond, find me again," she whispered. Her bloodstained lips opened a few times as if she would say more, but the life ebbed from her.

"Elspeth?" Fergus stared at her chest, waiting for it to rise. Just one more breath. One more word. One more kiss. One more moment. One more…

She didn't move.

Pain racked over him, crippling him with death's cruelty. This was not how it was meant to be. Seven years. That's all they'd had. They were supposed to have eternity.

"*Gráim thú*. I promise, Elspeth," Fergus whispered, gathering her into his arms. "Whatever lies ahead, I'll find ya."

Chapter Two

Green Vallis, Wisconsin, Modern Day

"Take cover, lads. We're under attack!"

At his nephew's shout, Fergus paused at the top of the broad marble staircase, looking down over the mansion's front hall just in time to see Euann darting in the front door. Euann was a young warlock, only four-hundred-and-some years old, so Fergus didn't take his nephew's warning too seriously. This was probably just another of his nephews' pranks.

"What have ya boys done this time?" Fergus asked. "Ya did not try to cast a snowball-fight spell again, did ya? Have ya learned nothing from the time ya enchanted the villagers?"

"It's worse." Euann dramatically latched the door shut and pressed his back to the wood. He wore a thick coat though one would hardly recognize it was winter by the consistent temperature inside the mansion home. "And for the record, that snowball fight succeeded. They worked out their demons and were too tired to start a war by the time it was over." Gesturing with his hands, he magickally forced the window shades to close without touching them.

"Date not go well?" Rory's voice drifted up from below, apparently unconcerned with Euann's plight. "We warned ya that girls don't like it when ya peep in their windows. They don't see it as charming, cousin. Now they call it stalking."

"It's Belladonna," Euann whispered. He held his arms out against the door like the devil might try to gain entrance. "She's back, and she's carrying."

Fergus frowned, wondering what could possibly cause a member of his clan to project such fear. After centuries, there wasn't much that could rile them—even when perhaps it should. They had just moved to Green Vallis, and the place did seem to be an epicenter of both power and danger, but all the real threats had been dealt with. They'd killed the *lidérc* threat and the local *bean nighe*. One was a psychic vampire. The other was a bringer of death. The odds that a third threat resided in mid-Wisconsin were highly unlikely.

He waited, listening and watching to see if he could detect trouble. The skies did not darken. The weather did not change. He leaned over the hundred-year-old oak banister and found Rory holding completely still midstride. Curious, he asked the boys, "Who is Belladonna?"

"Shh!" his nephews hissed in unison. Rory frantically waved his arms, as if doing so could force his uncle to remain quiet.

Seeing the look on Rory's face, Fergus relaxed some. After centuries of living, he was used to his family's antics. Unconcerned, he made his way down the stairs. The familiar feel of his leather satchel pressed against his hip like an old friend, gently reminding him of what he must do.

The centuries had turned his grief into a hollow pit inside his soul. A constant ache radiated from there, and time had not lessened his love or the depth of his loss. It had, however, lessened his hope. It was his family that kept him going. His nephews, representatives of the sons he would never have. His brothers and sisters, pains-in-the-arses who didn't let him disappear into a magickal vortex. Malina, the niece he'd promised to watch over.

"What are ya doing?" Euann whispered.

Fergus frowned. The answer should have been obvious. He was doing the same thing he'd done every day, every night, for over four hundred years. He was going to call his Elspeth to him. Someday, her soul would hear him. Someday, he'd find his answer. Someday, he would be with her again. He had to believe it because he had nothing else to believe.

Whatever is beyond, find me again.

He'd promised her.

Euann glanced down to the bag carrying the latest of Fergus's magickal concoctions as if answering his own question.

"Euann, why are ya trying to block your uncle from leaving?" Angus appeared carrying a giant roasted turkey leg. He pointed it at his son. "Stop playing around and pack a bag. You're going to New York to check our assets there."

"Why me?" Euann dropped his arms.

"Ya wanted to start the tech-whatever company," Angus said. "Their robots are sick, and they gave the workers a hacking cough. I will not be responsible for the end of mankind because ya want to play with—"

"Sick?" Euann frowned for a moment. "Hackers gave us a virus?"

"Isn't that what I said?" Angus took a bite of

the turkey leg. "Go and make sure everyone in the office has medical care."

"Computer virus," Euann stated.

"And shut down the cyborg army," Angus ordered. "If we want to end mankind, we'll use magick like respectable warlocks."

"I've told ya, they are not those kinds of robots. They are prototypes. We are designing medical equipment for third-world countries, and trying to develop lifelike cadavers for—" Euann attempted to explain.

"Hey, where'd that come from?" Rory interrupted, nodding at the turkey leg.

They all knew what the medical research lab was working on, but it was entertaining to frustrate Euann. At their age, they took their fun where they could get it.

"Malina is materializing food with Jane out of a Renaissance Faire catalog," Angus stated. "I'll tell ya lads one thing is certain. Dinner is much better now that we have Iain's little battery."

Angus referred to his nephew's new wife, Jane. She was a natural power source for their magick. Magick had to come from some place. That kind of energy didn't just appear out of nowhere. Although sex would work for a power surge, it wasn't a steady source. Typically, they borrowed energy from the environment. It was why they had moved to Wisconsin. Green Vallis was a strong place filled with nature. However, since Jane was half *bean nighe*, she acted like a power conduit, which kept them from killing trees, and enabled them to replenish nature.

"Belladonna comes. Hold down the fort, Euann, we're counting on ya to protect us all." Rory smirked and hurried into the dining room.

A soft knock sounded on the door. Angus again motioned for his son to get out of the way and moved as if he would open the door. Euann shook his head in denial and refused to leave his post.

The knock sounded again.

Angus zapped a little stream of magick at his son, shocking him just enough in the hip to get him to jump aside.

"Ow!" Euann protested. He returned fire, shooting a tiny stream of magick at his father. Angus laughed and darted from the room, still carrying the turkey leg.

Fergus sighed, curious to see the creature at the door.

"Uncle Fergus, no," Euann warned. "Do not let her in."

Drawing his hand behind him, he let a concentrated ball of magick equip his palm. His body tensed as he reached for the doorknob.

"It's your funeral," Euann said before running from the room.

Fergus wasn't sure what to expect, but it definitely wasn't the lovely woman holding a basket. He glanced behind her, confused. No zombie army. No hoard of bees. No legion of stray cats. Just a hillside covered with snow.

"Hi, neighbor." Her bubbly voice was incredibly pleasant. The sound took him by surprise. As did her smile. She looked nothing like his Elspeth, except for the line of her jaw. A lot of women had that jaw. He'd seen it numerous times over the years as he'd looked for pieces of Elspeth in every woman he came across. And each time he wanted to touch whatever piece of her resemblance he thought he'd found, just to see he if could feel his wife again. He refrained, not touching the visitor.

The jaw is where the similarities ended. The basket-wielding threat in front of him had dark auburn hair, not brown sun-streaked with blonde. Aye, hair could be dyed, but eyes could not. Her eyes were dark brown, not green. Plus, she was shorter and not willowy. No Elspeth here. Again. Even if his wife came back as someone else, he'd sense his magick inside her radiating back at him. He would know her soul. Of that, he was certain. Elspeth was his heart. He would know her when he saw her.

Fergus slowly squished the energy ball and drew his empty hand from behind his back. The cold winter air circled his naked legs beneath the kilt, but it didn't bother him. Behind him, the house stayed warm, the invisible barrier not letting the cold air in even as he held the physical door open. He again glanced over the expansive front lawn and long cobblestone driveway, trying to see why Euann had run. He sensed nothing in the outbuildings, nothing in the woods beyond the curve of the hill.

"I, ah, wanted to welcome you to the neighborhood," the woman said. She lifted the basket. "I hope your family is settling in nicely."

Fergus turned his gaze back to her. They had been in the neighborhood for months. It seemed a little late to have a welcoming committee stop by, and she was hardly the first to show up at their doorstep. Many of the townspeople were curious about the new Scottish clan living in the mansion on the hill overlooking Green Vallis.

Knitted gloves matched the woman's scarf and hat. Pink tinted her cheeks. She had nice eyes and an open smile. He found himself studying her face, wondering at the mystery behind her. How could she possibly be a threat? She seemed so genuine and kind. And lovely. Very, very lovely to look at.

A siren, perhaps? Fergus inhaled deeply. No, they were too far from Greek waters, and she didn't smell of saltwater and fish.

"Are those bagpipes I hear?" she asked, leaning to glance inside the home.

Fergus didn't hear anything. He gave a small shake of his head.

"Oh." She gestured the basket toward him. "So, ah, welcome?"

Slightly confused, he lifted the cloth napkin to look inside. Her smile widened, and he found himself reaching in to take out a small cookie.

"I baked them last night," she said. "I hope you like cookies."

There was something about the way she watched him, her eyes glancing from his hand to his mouth and back again. What else could he do but place the morsel in his mouth?

The flavor was unbearable. She'd somehow managed to combine salt, sugar and garlic with the texture of burnt and raw dough. His mouth full, he mumbled, "What kind of cookie is this?"

"Shortbread," she said.

"Shortbread," he mumbled in clarification, unable to force himself to swallow. It didn't taste like shortbread. The longer it sat in his mouth, the worse the flavor became.

"Oh, what a cute dog!" She leaned sideways to look past him at the staircase.

Fergus took the opportunity to turn and spit the cookie behind the front door where she couldn't see. He'd thought launching the food from his mouth would take care of the problem, but he couldn't have been more wrong. The horrid cookie was gone, but the salty-garlic-sugar taste remained in full force. In some ways, the air seemed to make the taste stronger.

"What's his name?" she asked.

He turned his attention to the out-of-breath English bulldog who labored his way down the stairs. "Traitor."

"Excuse me?"

"I call him Traitor."

There was a drawn out silence before she began to laugh. "Oh, Traitor, because you're Scottish, and he's English. How old is he?"

"Fifty-six," he stated.

"So...eight?"

"Fifty-six," he repeated, trying to lessen his accent for the American.

"People years. That makes him eight in dog years."

Fergus had no idea what she was talking about. He'd had Traitor for fifty-six years and was very attached to the creature. Traitor moved over to the discarded cookie and made slobbery noises as he licked at the floor.

"I love animals. You know, when I was a kid I used to have dreams that I was a dog chewing on leather. It was so real I'd wake up with the taste of it in my mouth," she said, conversationally.

Fergus arched a brow, unsure how to answer the comment. "I don't dream like that."

"Oh, yeah, I guess that's a weird anecdote to tell people when I first meet them." She gave a soft laugh and looked at him expectantly.

He found he didn't want to disappoint her. Unsure what he was supposed to do and fearing she just might try to feed him another of the monstrosities she called cookies, Fergus abruptly took the basket from her. She gasped softly in surprise but let it go.

"I guess I won't keep you," she said, her words measured and questioning, as if she wanted him to do something more.

"Aye," he answered.

"Oh, my name is Donna Montgomery. I live about a half block from the bottom of the hill. It's the house with the portrait studio sign out front. That's me. Local photographer."

Fergus could see why his nephews called her *Bella* Donna. She was very *bella*, beautiful. But since when did any single male member of his family run from an attractive woman?

He continued to stare at her. She didn't look like a succubus or an *empusa*, and the conditions were not right for her to be a *dziwozona*.

Donna gave a deliberate nod and inched away from him. "Have a great day, neighbor. Welcome, again, to the neighborhood."

"Aye," he repeated. He slowly shut the door on her.

As soon as the door latched, he dropped the basket and ran toward the dining room. He passed the long oak table where his nieces were magickally procuring festival food from magazine pictures. He hurried toward the library where the liquor supply was kept. Drinking whiskey straight out of the decanter, he let it burn the awful taste from his mouth.

"Wow," Euann said from behind him. "You're a smooth one, Ferg."

Fergus turned, still gulping down the hard liquor while he eyed his nephew. He pulled the decanter away from his lips. Breathing hard, he asked. "What do ya mean? I waited until she wasn't looking before I spit—"

"Belladonna clearly likes ya," Rory stated, joining Euann. "That was called flirting."

Fergus frowned. "Donna is *bella*, but I don't think—"

Rory laughed. "No, we call her *Belladonna* because she's been trying to poison us for two months with her cooking. Trust me, when you're expelling your guts in the bushes, her pretty loses its charm quickly."

"It is kind of her to try," Fergus defended, unsure why he bothered. He didn't know this woman and her cooking was indefensible. He took another swig of the whiskey, letting the liquid fill his mouth before swishing it between his teeth.

"Ya know, cousin, she never looked at me like that," Rory said to Euann.

"Me neither," Euann answered, also pretending Fergus wasn't standing before them. "I think she likes Uncle Fergus."

"Aye. Too bad a piece of driftwood has more skills than he does when it comes to women," Rory observed. "I couldn't tell if he was flirting back or trying to hex her."

"I did not flirt," Fergus stated. His nephews ignored him.

"Should we offer to help him?" Euann was barely able to keep the laugh out of his teasing voice. "I think Malina might have a little of that love potion Lydia used on Erik. We could take away Fergus's inhibitions. It worked for my big brother. He finally found a woman who will put up with him."

"Ach, no, I do not want to see Fergus shaking his naked arse on the front lawn." Rory gave a dramatic shiver. "Some images cannot be erased from my mind."

"I don't know. Erik's poetry was quite lovely," Euann said.

"But not his singing voice," Rory commented.

"I think ya boys have been sampling your Uncle Raibeart's liquor stash again," Fergus said louder. "I told ya, I did not flirt with that woman."

"Oh, aye, we know," Rory answered him. "What ya did was *far* from flirting. Yet she still seems to like ya."

"Even ya should have noted the way she smiled at ya, Uncle Ferg," Euann added. "She wanted ya to talk to her."

"I should inform her that I am married." Fergus decisively set the decanter down and made a move to leave. "I did not mean to give her the wrong impression."

"Go try the funnel cakes, laddies." Angus appeared, tugging on Rory and Euann's arms to yank them out of the room. When they were alone, Angus sighed and turned instantly serious. After a long moment, he said, "I miss her too, Fergus, but Elspeth would not want this life for ya. Perhaps we let it go on for too long, this pining of yours. I don't expect ya to find another Elspeth, but there is something to be said for companionship. If ya worry about hurting the woman's feelings, ya never need tell her ya carry another in your heart. No one expects ya to fall in love, but lust might be good for ya. And it sounds as if this Donna woman might have been stopping by in hopes of meeting ya. She probably saw ya around town and wanted an introduction."

"Ya would never betray your wife," Fergus said. "Why are ya telling me to betray mine?"

"Aye, I wouldn't. But this is not about me. If I could give Elspeth back to ya, I would. She died protecting my daughter. That is a debt no man can repay. All I can do is honor her, and try to think of what she would want for ya. Elspeth loved ya, brother, and that is how I know she would not want this eternity for ya. It has been over four hundred years. I think it's time we let Elspeth rest. I think it's time ya let yourself have even a brief moment of companionship. I don't know if a man can have more than one *fíorghrá* in his life, but ya can have a life."

"What makes ya think I'd even be interested in this Donna?" Fergus crossed his arms over his chest.

"That part is fairly obvious." Angus cleared his throat and glanced to Fergus's kilt.

Fergus looked down and was surprised to find his erection jutting forward. The bag he carried across his chest pressed the tartan down on his hip so that there was no hiding the way Donna affected him. Like a schoolboy, he instantly shoved the bag to hang in front of his waist.

Angus chuckled. "Just think about it. Oh, and your dog is eating the basket. Ya might want to take him outside. Traitor might be immortal thanks to your spells, but even I am sure he's not supposed to eat garlic. The whole front hall reeks of it."

Reminded of the taste, Fergus again grabbed the whiskey.

Chapter Three

Donna hummed softly to herself, smiling brightly for anyone to see as she made her way down the long MacGregor mansion drive. She didn't know the song, but it didn't matter. The bagpipes and violins in her head filled her spirit and made her happy. The world was a wonderful, glorious place, and today was a brilliant day.

What a nice man. She paused, realizing she didn't know the last Mr. MacGregor's name. He had kind eyes. Mr. Kind Eyes MacGregor. Such a friendly disposition too.

They really were an attractive family. She'd met most of them briefly—some in town, others when she'd dropped off her gifts. The genetic pool had been kind to them. Money and good breeding probably helped.

Good breeding? Did people still say good breeding? Donna wondered at the antiquated thought.

The snow crunched beneath her feet. She glanced back to see the mansion disappearing behind the snowy hill. The Georgian was so pretty and majestic, overlooking the town that sprawled over the valley on one side, with the forest on the other. The house had sat abandoned nearly her entire life, remaining dormant until the MacGregors purchased it several months before. Everyone in town knew the story of the displaced English lord who'd come to Wisconsin in disgrace to build the estate. Children used to dare each other to roam the gardens at night, telling stories of how the mansion was haunted. Then, as teenagers, young couples would sneak up to be alone. It was a constant backdrop to their small town life, a landmark. In a way, the people of the town had always looked up at that mansion and felt its dominating presence. Now, when they looked up, they thought of the MacGregor family.

"Such a nice family," she said to herself before humming again. "Such a nice man."

With each step, her smile dropped by the smallest degree and the song began to fade until she stood at the end of the drive on the slushy street. Suddenly, the cold seeped into her toes, as if only now her nerve endings worked. Her humming stopped, as did the music in her head.

Frowning in confusion, she looked up the drive. Her gaze followed her tracks. Did she just deliver…cookies? To the surly Scottish neighbor?

What the hell was wrong with her? Cookies? Fucking cookies?

Donna wasn't sure what was worse. The fact she couldn't remember why she'd felt compelled to deliver food to the neighbors. The fact this wasn't the first time it had happened. Or the fact no one should eat anything that came out of her kitchen. Ever. It should be illegal for her to even own an oven.

Why was she trying to feed the wealthy neighbors? It's not like they needed her charity. They were the town gazillion-something-aires. And, if she was so compelled to take them baked goods, why didn't she just go to the bakery and pick something up?

And what was with that last MacGregor guy? Like the others, he was handsome, maybe too handsome. The gray at his temples added the impression of wisdom. That same notion was reflected in his eyes. He had the face and body of a fantasy. The kilt didn't hurt that image either. Unfortunately, with his wise gaze had come a bit of a condescending annoyance when she'd spoken to him. He'd just stared at her, acting like everything that came out of her mouth was idiotic.

Well, to be fair, everything out her mouth *had* been idiotic.

Had she really told him the story of dreaming she was a dog chewing on shoes? It wasn't as if that was an anecdote she thought about often.

"Hi, I'm Donna. It's not like I have a furry fetish, but here's a random get-to-know-me fact. I used to vividly dream I was a dog." She sighed heavily as she grumbled to herself. "At least I didn't tell him about the flying insect dreams. Or my imaginary friend teaching me how to stick fight, and subsequently being rushed to the hospital to be psychologically evaluated."

Though really, what had her aging parents expected? She was an only child living on a farm in the middle of Nowhere, Iowa. She'd been a surprise pregnancy to a couple in their forties. Now her mother would have been one to bring baked goods to the new neighbors. That woman knew how to cook. Unfortunately, Donna had been too much of a tomboy to pay attention.

The jacket she wore wasn't meant for such cold temperatures. Donna hugged her arms over her chest and tucked her head down to continue the trek home. What was happening to her? She could recall every instance of going to the grocery store, reading recipes on her phone, staying up all night baking, putting the food items into cute little baskets to take up the hill. She had been doing it sporadically since late October, but she couldn't recall *why* she did it. Normally, when new people moved into town, she just sent a photography coupon out with the local welcome wagon lady and called it good.

Glancing up, she found a pretty woman staring at her from across the street. Brownish blonde waist-length hair blew in the breeze. Donna blinked and jumped back from the splashing puddle as a car zoomed past. When she again looked, the woman was gone. She searched up and down the now empty street before continuing home.

"Maybe my imaginary friend is all grown up and coming back to say hi. I should have her hit me over the head with the stick again, knock some sense into me."

Her house was small, nestled between the Johnstons and Mr. Reyer. It had a decent yard and a small porch. Her sidewalk was cleared of snow, which meant Mrs. Johnston had taken pity on her again and made Mr. Johnston get out his snow shovel.

The yellow siding and white trim guarded the sanctuary inside. This was her life, the piece she'd carved out for herself. She wasn't rich. She wasn't famous. Donna simply was. She wanted nothing to do with the new town nobles living above them. So it made no sense why she'd try to make friends with them.

Any farm-girl dreams she'd had of becoming spectacular had long faded. She'd found with adulthood that she really wasn't suited for photographing the Amazon jungle, or trekking through the wilds to discover isolated tribes. Instead, she traveled in books and photographed children and weddings. She had no desire for fame and fortune. People like the MacGregors lived in the spotlight. The rich always did. Donna liked to live behind the camera flash. She liked quiet. She liked normal.

So then why was she suddenly trying to be Suzie Homemaker for the new Scottish neighbors living as local celebrities in the mansion on the hill?

Donna opened her front door. It wasn't locked. Apparently, Baker Donna hadn't felt the need for personal security.

She closed the door and locked it before kicking off her wet shoes and dropping her gloves and hat on the floor. She then trudged toward her bedroom to get out of her wet clothes. At least her home was warm, even if it did smell of whatever painful concoction had come out of her oven.

"Comhstach."

Donna gasped at the soft whisper. She turned, ready to confront the man standing in her home. "Who's there?"

She reached for her pocket. Fucking wonderful. Neighborly Donna didn't believe in carrying her cell phone.

She held still for a long moment, listening to the silence. Nervously, she made her way down the hall. She pushed open a creaky door and switched on the bathroom light. No one was there. Next, she tried the extra bedroom that had been turned into her office. The computer monitors were dormant on the wood desk, and her camera equipment sat untouched. Inching toward her living room, which doubled as a showroom, she didn't notice anything out of the ordinary. Large photographs of happy faces stared from oversized frames. Her front door remained closed.

"Hello?" she called softly, going to check the kitchen. It was primarily used to store take-out containers but was now covered in discarded bakeware and a fine dusting of flour. One set of footprints in the flour led from where she'd baked toward the living room. The kitchen was empty, and yet she found herself going toward the counter.

A handprint had been pressed into the flour mess. Donna glanced at her hands. They were still red from being outside with insufficient gloves. Slowly, she lowered her palm over the print. Her fingers were too long to fit inside the mark.

"What is happening to me?" she whispered.

Chapter Four

"What do ya think? Angus says lust would be good for me, but what do I know of courting these modern women?" Fergus took a deep breath. Part of him was very interested in the idea of slaking his lust with Donna. She'd been in his head since he'd first met her. The attraction he had for the woman was very strong, stirring in his body as nothing had in a very long time. "I don't know why I'm even thinking about it. Ya know what I'm going to say, don't ya? My Elspeth. I've never cheated on her."

The ache was real and always there. It would never go away.

But perhaps the others were right. He'd failed to bring Elspeth back. Every day for over four hundred years, he had tried, and he had failed. There were no more spells to attempt. There hadn't been for decades, centuries. Now he was just making things up, killing trees to fuel his magick so he could recite a new version of an old spell. He'd opened portals. He'd done shady deals with even shadier necromancers. He'd spilled blood and tears. He had nothing left.

He lay on his stomach on the floor of his bedroom, his face a foot from the English bull-dog's wrinkled smile. Traitor stared into his eyes as if enthralled by his words, but Fergus knew the dog wouldn't answer him.

"I've managed to keep ya alive, haven't I, friend? Years of trying has taught me much, but it has not taught me how to talk to a woman."

The dog wobbled forward on his stomach and licked Fergus's face with his thick tongue.

"Ya like her, don't ya? Ate all those cookies she brought by."

Traitor burped and continued to breathe hard.

Fergus grimaced and pushed up from his stomach. "Ya make a good point. I should return her basket. My nephews were not too kind to her. That's no way to behave in a new town, and gifts should be reciprocated. We want to make a good impression."

Traitor snorted.

"Ya don't know what ya are talking about. I go for the clan, to make a good impression."

Traitor rolled onto his back and began twitching back and forth to scratch himself on the thick carpet.

"Do not judge me." Fergus glanced down over his slacks. Little white strands of fur stuck to them. With a magickal brush of his hand, he cleaned them off as he left the room to search out his niece. Malina would be able to help him with the gift basket. Fergus didn't know much about hair ribbons, baubles, trinkets and the like. Any gift he put together would include a bottle of whiskey and golf balls. Did most women like a good whiskey?

"Malina," Fergus called loudly as he came down the stairs. "I need ya to get me girl products."

Malina stood in the front hall with Euann and Rory. All three turned in unison to look at him.

Euann had a packed duffle bag on the floor beside him, clearly getting ready to leave for New York. "I warned ya if ya didn't use it your manhood would fall off."

"I don't think tampons are going to help ya, Uncle Fergus," Rory teased. "Unless another of your spells went incredibly wrong."

"I don't understand ya, laddies. Why would I

need to *tampion* something?" Fergus frowned. He had no reason to stuff a rag into a hole. "Can't ya magickally stuff something into—"

Rory and Euann began to laugh harder.

Fergus didn't understand why they thought plugging was so funny. "I was asking for help making a present to give Donna to thank her for her generosity in welcoming our family. Unless ya think she'd like a bottle of my favorite whiskey?"

"Ignore Euann," Malina said, her English accent a contrast to her brother. "I will help you."

"Aye, ignore me," Euann stated. "We'll all help ya put together the perfect gift. Trust us, we know what women like."

"Aye," Rory agreed. "The perfect gift. Ya are right, Fergus. We need to be more neighborly."

"Good." He nodded. That was more like the mature attitude he expected from them.

Chapter Five

"Comhstach."

"I can't hear you. I can't hear you," Donna repeated to herself, ignoring the man's whisper. No one was there, only a voice. Sometimes she understood the half sentences. Mostly, the words were in some Celtic language she didn't speak. She guessed Scottish Gaelic, but she really had no way of knowing. Each time they made her tremble, part with dread, part with curiosity, always with anticipation.

Donna took a deep breath and set down her camera as it synced Misty Wallace's senior pictures onto the computer. Without much thought, she walked toward the front door and opened it.

A MacGregor man stood, his hand lifted as if to knock. She frowned, recognizing him as the one who'd accepted her cookies and then given her short, grumpy answers. How could she have thought he was nice? The more she'd played the scene in her head, the more she felt like a simpering idiot, and the more she became convinced this particular MacGregor lacked all charm and was a jerk. To see him at her front door, hand suspended in mid-air and a smile on his face, was bizarre to say the least.

"What do you want?" Donna didn't intend the question to come out as harshly as it sounded, but having him on her front porch caused a small shiver to wash over her. He was much more hand-some than she'd remembered. The expression in his dark eyes reminded her of lost moments—an innocent searching she hadn't felt since she was nine years old, a strong cup of coffee on a cold early morning, the angst of being a teen, the smell of her grandmother's baking on a childhood after-noon, the sorrow of losing a pet, the happiness of capturing the perfect instant on film. The depths of his gaze mesmerized her, and she felt light-headed. The impressions from the past became vivid, a waking dream full of sound and scents in no chronological order. He blinked and looked away. The rush of feelings inside her subsided as if they'd never been, leaving her feeling emptier than before.

His expression fell, and he dropped his hand. "Ya do not sound the same as before."

The resonance of his voice brought her fully back into the moment. Donna arched a brow. So she didn't sound like a bubbly airhead? He didn't exactly sound like the arrogant asshole. "Neither do you."

"I wanted to thank ya for your welcome." He held up her cookie basket. "My family put this together for ya."

"*Comhstach*," the Scottish voice whispered in hushed determination, so soft it could have been her mind playing tricks on her.

Donna didn't readily take the gift. She was afraid to reach toward him. Her hands shook. There was something all too familiar about this situation. "I don't think we've officially met. I'm Donna."

"Aye, Donna Montgomery, so ya said." Like the rest of the MacGregors she had encountered, he had dark hair and sensual eyes and a natural sex appeal, but there was something special about him that set him apart from the others. She couldn't place it. The idea was more of a feeling than a logical fact.

"And you've never said." She couldn't help her

small smile. "Do you have a name?"

"Oh, Fergus MacGregor," he answered. "Sorry, I'm not used to talking."

"Silent type, eh, Gus?" Donna chuckled. She held out her hand, finally willing to accept the basket. It was a lot heavier than when she'd delivered it. A chilly breeze whipped over her shoulder as if originating from inside the warm house. She looked behind her to find the source of the strange draft and said, "It's cold. Please, come in."

Donna stepped aside and let Fergus pass. He paused in the entryway and looked around at her giant photo displays. "Ya must really like your family."

Donna laughed. "They're my customers."

"Ya must really like your customers."

"Some of them," Donna answered, thinking of Misty Wallace's photo shoot processing onto her computer. The girl was as snooty as her mother and lacked all natural ability to smile…or say anything nice. "Others not so much, but I do love my job." Noticing the boxes on her floor, she quickly slid them aside with her foot and added, "Sorry, let me just get those out of your way. I'm photographing the Annual Winter Skate and my display setups seem to overtake everything if I'm not careful."

"Winter Skate?"

"Town tradition for the holidays. There's a festival, and everyone skates the creek through the woods."

"Which woods?"

"Oh." Donna frowned. "I guess that would be through your woods now."

"The townsfolk plan to trespass on our land?"

Donna pretended to study her hand. There was the arrogant tone she remembered from their first meeting. He apparently wasn't too keen on the idea of the common people on his noble estate. She sighed, biting down the urge to say her sarcastic thoughts aloud. "Is this the first you're hearing of it? I hope it's not a problem. The town does it every year, and no one has lived in the mansion, so it has never been an issue, but I suppose… You should talk to the city council. I'm sure they'll know all the permits and details and whatnot."

"We will do that."

Donna hoped they didn't cancel the celebration. The yearly gig really was an excellent source of holiday income. Not to mention, it was a nice tradition.

He didn't speak, merely stared at her as if he wanted her to continue talking.

"*Comhstach*," the Scottish voice in her mind stated louder, tickling her thoughts as if she was supposed to be remembering something critically important. It was probably something from a television show, some stupid line that she couldn't get out of her head.

"*Comhsta…*" she repeated softly to herself as if saying the word might help produce the meaning.

Fergus colored slightly. "I'm sorry, did ya just call me a…?"

She blinked, realizing she'd started paying attention to the voice in her head instead of the man in front of her. "What? Oh, no, sorry, it's just this thing that I've been trying to remember. It has been driving me crazy."

"It sounds like you're attempting to say *comhstach*."

"You've heard of it?" Donna asked in surprise.

"Aye. It means whore."

"Oh." Donna bit her lip. So apparently the voices in her head were calling her a whore? They must be able to see the very unladylike thoughts playing in her mind about Mr. Fergus MacGregor. "Never mind. That can't be what I'm trying to recall. Anyway…"

She glanced uncomfortably around the room and then remembered the present. Glad to have a distraction, she pulled at the cloth covering the basket to open her gift. Setting it down on the couch, she reached inside to retrieve a stack of books. Donna read the titles aloud, "*How to Cook 101. Does Everything You Make Stink? Cooking for Chronic Burners. Stop Poisoning Your Friends and Family in Ten Easy Steps.*" Under the books was a stack of takeout gift cards. "Fast food cards? Is this a joke?"

"We wanted to…" Fergus coughed nervously. "My family…gift…neighbor…should go."

Fergus turned to leave. Donna dropped the books onto the couch and followed him outside. She didn't wear a coat and the winter wind whipped over her. She had tried to be polite, tried to give him the benefit of the doubt, but this was too insulting.

"I get it. I'm a bad cook. I wouldn't blame you if you quietly threw away everything I brought up to you. But that gift you gave me? And getting upset about a winter festival? And that rude way you greeted me when I came to your door? You are kind of a jerk, Mr. MacGregor. Do you think because you're rich you can breeze into town and do whatever you want? Treat people like this? I mean, sure I shouldn't have brought you food. I don't even know why I tried. But it wasn't done with malice. I didn't deserve your family running away from me and slamming the door in my face.

Yeah, I gave Euann the benefit of the doubt and pretended that wasn't what happened, but I think it's pretty obvious now. And I surely don't deserve such a spiteful gift."

Fergus didn't speak.

Donna's chest tightened. The MacGregor insult stung. They didn't know her. The gift was just mean. She felt tears burning the back of her eyes. "You know what, never mind. I'm sorry I even bothered." She pointed at a white sheepdog sitting on the sidewalk watching them. "Welcome to Green Vallis. That dog appears to be waiting for you. You should take him and go home. Don't worry, you won't see me at your doorstep again, and I won't try to talk to you."

FERGUS DIDN'T KNOW what to say or do. What did he know about women? He'd never been suave. The fates had taken pity on him when they'd sent him Elspeth.

He should have looked in the basket before handing it to her. It wasn't a surprise that his family had done something stupid. They'd think it was a funny prank. Donna wasn't laughing.

A wave of sadness passed over him, her

sadness. He finally glanced to where she pointed, but Traitor wasn't there. No dog was.

When his attention was turned, she'd slipped back inside. Before he knew what he was doing, he followed her. She gasped as he pushed open her door while she tried to close it. "What—"

Fergus cupped her face in his hands and kissed her. He wasn't sure what had come over him. Donna was sad, and the idea that he'd caused it forced him to act. It had been a long time since he'd kissed a woman, and at first he didn't move his mouth. He just held his lips to hers. When he pulled away, she was breathing heavily.

"Wha…at?" Donna reached for his face and pulled his mouth to hers. Her lips moved against his, kissing passionately. Despite the years of celibacy, the feel of her drew up the primal instinct to respond. He moaned, pulling her body against his. A myriad of emotions whirled inside him, but they were all drowned out by a rampant desire. The mindlessness of the moment took hold of them. Magick swirled in his veins, leaking from his fingertips into her skin. He couldn't stop it.

Donna pulled away and whispered, "Why did you do that?"

"I say things wrong. None of my spells work," he answered honestly.

"Spells?" Donna gave him a dazed smile. He saw his magick dancing in her eyes. "I'm not as complicated as all that. Though I will give you this much, you have a very strange way of asking a woman out."

"Out where?" he asked, confused.

"Dinner?" She smiled, and he couldn't look away from her mouth. Her lips seemed swollen from where he'd pressed into them. "If I promise not to cook it?"

"My family should not have insulted ya."

"Is that your sheepdog? It looked like it followed you here. It's cold today. Should he come inside?" Donna leaned to look out of the open door.

"What dog?"

"Standing by that woman," she said.

Fergus didn't see any woman or dog. "I think the light is blinding ya, lass."

"Huh, must be."

Fergus was used to magick being a big part of his life. But to see it now staring back at him from her eyes made him unsure about how to proceed. His nephews had caused a lot of problems in their own relationships by using magick. Then again, he wasn't looking for true love. He'd had his shot at true love and had watched that love die in his arms. That reminder was like a cold splash of water.

As much as he wanted Donna, Fergus knew he shouldn't be doing this. Donna's taste was still on his mouth. He wanted nothing more than to keep kissing her. No, that wasn't true. How could he think that? He wanted nothing more than to get his wife back.

Elspeth was his everything.

What was he doing here? This wasn't right.

It felt right. Donna felt right.

What am I doing? What am I doing?

Fergus realized he'd said nothing and was simply staring at the woman. The daze of his magick in her eyes begged him to continue. He wanted to continue. He needed to go. He wanted to stay. He wanted his wife. He wanted Donna.

Guilt warred with passion.

"Perhaps I should go," Fergus whispered.

Donna blinked slowly. "Perhaps you should stay."

It took all of his willpower to release her arms from his grip. "I have…family…ya…aye."

Fergus practically ran from Donna's house as if demons chased him. He didn't stop until he was back in his bedroom. Traitor had barely moved since he'd left. The dog lifted his head, and his big, wide mouth seemed to smile knowingly.

"Don't look at me like that. I didn't run away. I have to summon Elspeth," Fergus said.

Traitor grunted.

"What do ya know about it?" Fergus mumbled. He fell onto the bed, refusing to touch the sensitive mass of his erection as a punishment for what he'd almost done.

Chapter Six

Donna could not keep the smile off her face as she made her way up the hillside to the MacGregor mansion. Her latest gift basket hung on the crook of her arm. All was right with the world. The snow was perfect and evenly spread across the slope of the hillside. She had a date with a sexy Scotsman. Well, they hadn't confirmed an actual time and place yet, but she had a date sometime in the future.

She hummed softly to herself. The crunch of her shoes against the snowy cobblestone drive punctuated each step. Muddy tracks from numerous car tires led the way. As if on instinct, she reached for her camera and took several shots of the mansion on the hill. It wasn't as if she didn't have a thousand photographs of the house already, but today's somehow seemed better. Holding the camera in one hand and the basket in the other, she continued the climb.

The sound of laughter caught her attention. She turned her steps toward the side of the house to investigate further. Gaelic shouts became all the more pronounced. She couldn't understand most of the good-natured teasing, but the tone of the MacGregor voices indicated they were having a good time.

Without thought, Donna went to join them. For whatever reason, it seemed natural that she should do so. Her walk took her in the direction of the sounds emanating from the steep part of the hill that jutted toward downtown Green Vallis.

"Ach, I'm freezing my balls off!" someone shouted.

"Quit whining like a wee baby, Murdoch. Ya lost the last round, and now ya must pay the price with the rest of us."

"Shut it, Angus! That is because ya enchanted my log," the protesting Murdoch answered.

"And that is why ya are not the only one freezing your man bits off," Angus said.

"Ya know enchanting objects never goes well," a woman said with a touch of censure as if lecturing a naughty child. "It's no surprise his log flew a hard line for your arse."

"Oh, no, I do not want to hear about Angus's arse," Murdoch complained.

"Ya both are whining like wee babes." Donna's steps faltered at the sound of Fergus's strong voice. "Get those naked arses on the sleds or forfeit the title to me."

A shiver of anticipation washed over her. She had been able to think of little else since he'd kissed her. She'd waited for him to come back—hoping, praying, begging the fates to deliver him to her doorstep. When he hadn't visited, she'd decided to go to him.

Well, to be more exact, she'd decided to go to the grocery store, buy supplies, bake more cookies, and then come to him.

"Let the MacGregor Winter Games begin," a loud shout proclaimed just as Donna came around the corner of the house. Three naked MacGregor men raced snow sleds down the side of the steep hill. She recognized them as Angus, Murdoch, and Fergus. A gathering of family members stood behind the contestants, cheering them on. Her eyes followed Fergus in the lead.

The stupidity of the moment was not lost on Donna. The route they took was hardly safe, and the temperatures were such that they would be sure to catch cold from exposure. None of these things seem to concern the MacGregors though.

The photographer inside her instantly lifted the camera and began to shoot, even as the woman inside her blushed at the sight of grown men holding their manhoods and barreling toward the forest trees. Her lens zoomed in on Fergus, and she chuckled to herself. He looked happy, a wide smile across his face. Suddenly, a flash of light passed over the viewfinder. She pulled it away from her eye. Another couple of flashes shot out, moving from Fergus's hand toward the other sleds. Snow seemed to explode from the ground as if hit by a grenade.

Donna jolted in alarm. Fireworks? She lifted the camera to try to catch what was happening, but the men were farther from view. A shot hit Fergus in the arm, and he fell off his sled, somersaulting in the snow as the other two men disappeared behind the tree line.

Donna dropped the basket and ran toward the fallen man. The camera strap across her chest kept her from losing the equipment. Her feet slid, but she kept running.

"Gus?" she called when he didn't move. At the speed they'd been traveling, he would surely be injured without protection. "Gus!"

She arrived moments before the others. Donna kneeled on the ground beside Fergus. He wasn't moving. The siblings Malina and Iain, their cousin Rory, along with the supposed parental figures in the house—naked Angus with his wife, Margareta, and naked Murdoch with his wife, Cait—came to stand above her. Donna's heart hammered as fear overtook her. She didn't think, only reacted. The crimson red of blood stained the white snow, a horrifically telling contrast that all was not well. She moved her hands over the length of his naked body as if getting the nerve to go near the source of his main wound. She soon discovered his forearm was broken when she tried to lift it up from the snow. The bone had pierced through the skin. Fergus groaned softly. She instantly let go.

"What were you guys thinking?" Donna demanded. Why weren't they rushing to get him to the hospital?

"Dammit, Iain! How is she here? I thought ya said the security was in place." Angus didn't bother to retrieve his clothing. The cold didn't seem to trouble him.

"It is. I checked it myself this morning after Jane and Lydia left to take Charlotte holiday shopping." Iain appeared confused. "I don't know how she slipped in without us knowing. Euann reinforced all of the protection spells before he left."

"Fight about this later. Your brother needs help, Angus." Margareta MacGregor was a petite thing, but the way she looked up at her husband denoted who was in charge of that relationship.

"What do ya want me to do?" Angus asked. "He is the dumbass who fell off the sled."

"You shot him!" Donna exclaimed. Were these people crazy or just stupid? "We need to get him to a hospital. Someone call an ambulance. Help me get him out of the snow. Now."

"Leave it to my Cait," Murdoch interjected. He motioned to his wife.

Donna frowned. What was Cait going to do? Bake a casserole? She looked like a 1950s magazine cover housewife.

"What about her?" Iain eyed Donna.

"What about me?" Donna demanded.

"She called him Gus," Margareta said. The others didn't answer the strange observation.

"It's short for Fergus," Donna mumbled absently, unsure why such a thing would be worth commenting on.

"Are ya magick, lassie?" Angus crouched beside his brother to study her face. He slowly reached for her cheek. Donna wanted to pull away but couldn't. Cool fingers touched her skin. His gaze stared directly into hers. It tingled where he touched her as if he physically tried to pull some truth out of her. "Did Fergus tell ya about us?"

"There," Margareta motioned to her face. "Her eyes."

Angus sighed and dropped his hand. "Aye. She has Fergus's magick in her."

"Another *inthrall* like Lydia?" Iain asked.

"Lydia Barratt, who married your brother?" Donna tried to follow what they were talking about. They didn't answer her. She looked at the broken arm and then back to the family. What was going on here? "What's an *inthrall*?"

"Someone who can take our power," Malina answered.

"Malina," Margareta scolded.

"What, Ma? You're going to make Niall and I erase her memory of this anyway." Malina shrugged.

"First things first." Cait kneeled beside Fergus and placed her fingers on his arm. Donna stood and stepped away as the woman's hands began to glow. A nearby evergreen made a strange creaking noise. The tree's needles turned brown and started to rain gently onto the ground. The wound healed beneath Cait's hands.

"How...?" Donna shook her head. Cait placed her glowing fingers around Fergus's neck. His eyelids fluttered as he awoke.

"Ach, ya cheated! I call for another challenge,"

Fergus protested, not really looking at anyone in particular.

"Ya cannot call a challenge over an official challenge," Angus denied.

Fergus groaned. "How long did ya let me lie here, Cait? My arse is frozen to the ground."

Cait cleared her throat and looked up at Donna. Fergus followed the woman's gaze. His smile fell some. "Donna?"

"Gus," she said, the word hardly audible. He pushed up from the ground, no longer injured. Cait kicked white snow over the bloodstain to hide it.

He glanced around at his family. "How much did she see?"

"She knows," Angus said.

"She's shaking," Cait observed. "Let's get her inside. Iain, ya better check the border spells just in case. We don't want any more locals wandering up here undetected."

"Aye," Iain motioned to Rory. "Come help me."

"I'll help too," Malina stated, as if not wanting to be left out.

Donna wasn't sure what was happening. "What do I know?"

"Magick is real," Malina answered as she walked away.

"Malina!" Margareta reprimanded.

"We're warlocks," Malina added, clearly wishing to annoy her mother.

"Warlocks?" Donna repeated.

"Aye," Fergus said. "What ya saw was just a little bit of magick. Nothing to be afraid of. It's as natural as—"

"Flying balls of light coming out of finger-tips?" Donna inserted skeptically.

Fergus gave a small smile. "That's natural enough to us. Just like breathing is natural enough to ya. It's nothing to be worried about."

"Get her inside," Cait ordered Fergus.

"Come, Donna." Fergus took her by her arm and led her toward the house.

"What did Malina mean when she said she was going to erase me?" Donna asked.

"Don't worry about that. I promise, none of them are going to do anything to ya," he said.

She wasn't sure how they traveled so fast, but before she knew it they were in the front hall.

Bright dots of light danced before her, and for a moment she thought it was magick. Her eyes focused, and she realized they were holiday lights on a fifteen-foot Christmas tree. It appeared as if someone had hired a professional decorator to stage the home. "That's amazing decorating work. I would love to set up a photo shoot here. Everything you've done to restore this home is beautiful."

"The tree is Cait's doing." Fergus led her up the wide staircase to the second story.

"She has a lot of skill."

"It takes her three seconds," Fergus admitted. "She has my niece materialize the decorations from magazine pictures." He stopped and opened a door. Light from the room shone over his form, drawing attention to his muscular body. "Should I not say such things to ya? I don't want ya scared by talk of magick."

"Do I look scared?"

"No, but I think most in your position would be."

"I don't feel scared. I feel…" Donna looked him over, a little dazed. "You're naked."

"Aye." He opened the door wider to let her inside the room.

Donna glanced in. "That's a bedroom. You're naked, and that's a bedroom."

"Aye." Fergus grinned.

She let loose a long breath. "Good."

Chapter Seven

Fergus hadn't expected Donna to kiss him. Mortals normally couldn't handle learning about magick. The old witch trials were proof enough of that.

The shock of female hands against his naked flesh made him forget reason. He wanted her terribly, was starved for intimate contact. The ache inside him unfurled from a place of longing and denial. His mind focused on the soft glide of her touch over his chest. He couldn't have stopped her if he wanted to. The woman held him spell-bound more so than pure magick ever could.

The cold plastic of the camera body bumped into him, and the reality of it pulled him from his daze. Donna leaned back. Her heavy breath punctuated the air between them. She lifted the camera strap over her head and set the equipment on the floor. "Why are you in my head?"

"I think…" Fergus didn't really have an answer. "I think maybe ya are under a spell? Or ya absorbed my magick? That is why you're not frightened by the knowledge of my clan."

"Or there is something very real between us. I don't feel as if I should be frightened. I feel as if this is all meant to be happening." Donna touched his face and trailed her finger over his lip. "I haven't been able to think of anything else since you kissed me. I blew a photo shoot this morning because I was up all night baking you cookies. I honestly don't know why I keep trying to bake. It's like some strange urge overtakes me and I'm suddenly standing in front of the oven. Even now, there is something in me that wants to feed you."

"Do ya like me or are ya trying to kill me, lassie?" he teased.

"I'm not sure. Kiss me again and we'll find out." Donna didn't wait for him to obey her request. She pulled his face to hers and kissed him.

Fergus let his magick roll out of him and over her. Though centuries had passed since he'd been with a woman, some instincts remained. In many ways, it was as if time had not progressed. The primal feelings were as real as the day he'd suppressed them. Donna's kiss woke him up inside, feeding his hungry soul and arousing his dead heart.

Her clothing melted from her body, pooling around her feet. She gave a small gasp as he ran his hands down her naked sides. Magick heated his fingertips and small trails of blue light spread over her flesh. It tingled between them, connecting them. If their bodies pulled away from each other threads of light kept them joined.

"I want to make love to ya," he whispered.

"I thought that is what you were doing," she answered playfully.

Still, Fergus needed to be respectful and honest. "I can't marry ya, lass."

The words caused a flow of emotions inside him. He hated the honesty in them.

"I respect that," Donna said. "I didn't think this was a proposal."

MARRIAGE WAS the last thing on Donna's mind though she could easily admit she didn't really like hearing the statement. Her head swirled with a combination of desire and intrigue. She looked down to where his magick joined their chests and shoulders. It moved in pulsing threads of soft light between them. The sensation was like nothing she'd ever felt.

When she looked into his eyes, she didn't fear him. She was apprehensive of the unknown, of a world of magick and warlocks, but she didn't fear him. Ever since she was a girl, she'd believed in the unseen, had daydreamed of fairies dancing along fence posts, and trolls living at the bottom of the old well. Until now, she hadn't had any proof, but she'd always felt there was more to the world than science could explain.

As to sex, she was hardly a prude. She had felt the pull of him from that very first moment, a magnetic force that had drawn her to his home, and then to him. A logical mind could analyze what was happening. A fearful heart could find reason to run. Donna couldn't think logically, and her heart was not filled with fear.

Touching him felt right as if the joining of flesh was what the universe wanted. A dormant piece of herself awoke in a rush of adrenaline. Kissing him was like jumping off a cliff. Touching him was like being beneath a magickal waterfall. Her heart beat a hard rhythm.

Donna took his hand and led him to the bed. She could feel the desire in him as if it were her own. He wanted her but was holding back.

"I want this," she whispered between kisses. "I want you."

In that instant, his hands went from hesitant to bold. She made a small sound of surprise as he lifted her up and tossed her on the bed. Within seconds, he was climbing over her. The firm mattress molded along her back as she was pressed into its depths. The glide of flesh against flesh, aided by his powers, cocooned her in pleasure. Nothing outside of this moment mattered. Fragmented thoughts filtered through her mind— the flash of her camera, the sound of a horse's hooves, the clang of metal, a distant shout. Some of the images made little sense, and she could only assume they somehow came from him.

A deep ache filled her with longing until they were both desperately trying to join. She needed him and felt his need for her. Strands of blue and gold moved over his pupils as he stared into her eyes. It seemed a very long moment before he brought his arousal to brush against her. Seconds ticked by like minutes.

"I want to savor ya," he whispered.

"You think too much, Gus," she answered.

"Aye, so I've been told."

Donna pushed his shoulder and forced him onto his back. She straddled his waist, bringing his erection against her sex. Unlike him, she did not slowly savor the moment. She took it hard and fast, fulfilling the desperation growing inside her.

Donna impaled herself on his shaft. He groaned, grabbing her hips to keep her moving on top of him. The magick trails left their skin, floating above them like Northern Lights along the bedroom ceiling. The rhythm of their bodies continued, the movement undulating the current of the lights like waves on the ocean surface.

Color reflected over his handsome face and muscled chest. He skimmed his hands over her breasts and hips, touching as much as he could reach. She rocked faster, the pleasure building. Donna pressed her hands to his chest, steadying herself as she leaned in for another kiss. He slipped his tongue past her lips, triggering their release. She came hard, tensing and jerking with uncompromising force.

She collapsed onto the bed next to him as the tremors subsided. The lights over them began to fade. "I think I can get used to this magick thing, Gus."

"What makes ya call me that, lass?"

"Gus?" She chuckled. "I'm not sure. You just seem like a Gus to me. Do you mind?"

"No, call me whatever ya like."

Chapter Eight

Donna's mind drifted with thoughts as she lay between wake and sleep. Fergus kept her locked in his naked embrace, his muscles tightening anytime she moved as if he was worried she would leave him. Sexual release had brought deep relaxation. Her active mind quieted. Her bones felt like liquid encased in sedated muscles.

"What is a challenge on a challenge, and why can't you make one?" she asked.

"Ya just learned there is magick in the world, and *that* is the question ya have for me?" Fergus skimmed his fingers over her hip.

Donna chuckled. "Yeah."

"The MacGregor games have been going on for a long while now. Sporting events are whatever the terrain and weather allow. There are very few rules, but if ya use magick and it goes awry, a side challenge is wagered before everyone can continue on with the game. If ya don't do it, ya do not advance. I will not explain the point system to ya, but there is an enchanted scroll where the tally is kept. When the games started nearly three hundred years ago, we had no limit on the number of official side challenges as they related to the game, until side challenges became side challenges, which became more side challenges. The main game was never played, and the points could not advance. So about two hundred years ago, Cait decreed no more than one level of official side challenges. Unofficial wagers can be issued at any time by any MacGregor and are more or less like challenges."

"Did you just say Cait is over two hundred years old?" That piece of knowledge caused Donna's relaxed body to awaken fully, and she sat up on the bed. Being naked in front of him didn't bother her. The movement caused the covers to slide down his chest.

"She is not that young, but I'll be sure to tell her ya think so. Women seem to enjoy the idea of their youth." Fergus wrapped his fingers around her forearm to keep her from moving farther away from him.

Donna accepted his answer. The breadth of

his family, of history and time, made her feel very small. "And how old are you?"

"My nephews would say I was born at the dawn of time."

"So..." She studied his handsome face. He looked mid-thirties, possibly forties at the oldest. "What? You're like a thousand?"

"Och, no." Fergus laughed. "A little over seven."

"Seven hundred?"

He nodded.

She continued to stare, waiting for him to make some kind of indication he was joking. He did not. Donna hummed softly. "So I guess that would make us a May-December romance?" She gave a small laugh. "More like a BC-AD romance."

He arched a brow.

"BC-AD. Before Christ-*Anno Domini*?" She clarified. "As in dates. Like the year 456 BC."

"Oh, I understood, lass, but it was cute to watch ya mind work as ya tried to explain it." Fergus chuckled. He reached a finger to trace the bottom curve of her breast.

"You could at least pretend I'm funny." Donna hit him lightly on the leg. "So what other kinds of challenges do you issue?"

"Ya saw naked sledding. There's naked rafting,

boxing, caber tossing, haggis tossing, brother hurl-ing, shinty, curling, pub crawling, cheese rolling, levitation…" He chuckled. "Though, as I said, a MacGregor challenge can be called anytime inspi-ration strikes a family member. The last wager was a cake eating competition that involved males against females. The men won."

"That hardly seems fair," Donna observed. "I've only seen three females, and there's what? Like a hundred of you MacGregor males living here?"

"We are a large family, to be sure, though not quite a full hundred. The clan likes to stick together. It's safer that way. I like this house. It's big enough that if my nephews and nieces finally marry, they can being their partners here."

"Your brothers are married. Why aren't you?" She knew the question was a little prying, but that didn't stop her from asking it.

"Raibeart is not married," Fergus said.

"Who?"

"My oldest brother."

Donna studied his face. She ran her hand up the center of his chest and then back down again to rest on his stomach. "You said you couldn't marry me." Suddenly feeling very exposed, she pulled the bedding to cover her naked body. "It's because you already have a wife, isn't it?" She moved away from him, taking the covers with her as she stood by the bed. "That's it, isn't it? The reason you were surly toward me. You didn't want to be attracted to me because you're married."

Fergus didn't speak.

"What's her name?" Donna felt a little sick. She believed in the sanctity of relationships and had never been with a married man.

"Elspeth," he whispered.

Elspeth.

The single word kicked her in the gut.

Donna couldn't look at him. All the happiness from the moments before drained out of her limbs to leave her tense. Her chest ached, a stabbing, sharp pain that did not lessen with deep breaths. "Where is she?"

"I buried her along the border of England and Scotland in the winter of 1591."

Donna closed her eyes. The fact she wasn't the other woman should make her feel better, but in reality, what he said was much worse. She would have a chance against a living woman, but a ghost he'd been holding on to for hundreds of years? No. There was no competing against that kind of memory. The fact he still said he was married meant his heart was trapped.

"Tell me about her?" Donna whispered. Why was she torturing herself? The ache grew worse.

She found she couldn't move. She merely stood wrapped in the bedding that smelled of him.

"She was lovely, untarnished. One of those souls that instantly knew the right thing to do no matter how hard it was. She was always smiling. She loved the kitchen. Everyone loved it when she cooked. People would make excuses to come by the house during meal times. No matter how little she had for her pot, she would always share it."

At that, Donna glanced at him, feeling the comparison. "She sounds perfect."

"Aye, she was for me. She also had a stubborn streak and a bit of a jealous temper. She knew I would never betray her, and yet she'd glare down any woman who dared look at me too long."

"I'm sorry you lost her. May I ask how?" When he didn't speak, she nodded. "I understand. You don't have to talk about it."

Donna found her clothes on the floor where he'd magickally placed them. She grabbed her underwear and jeans and pulled them both up at the same time. The denim was hard where she'd kneeled in the snow, but they had dried as she'd dozed in his arms.

"It was during the height of the North Berwick witch trials. Malina was a baby. She'd been born with what they called the witch's mark. People were desperate then—for food, for salvation, to prove their piety and waive suspicions of witchcraft from themselves. There were many reasons for someone to name a child to the authorities if they believed that child was touched by the devil. Confessions were extorted with torture. People would say anything to avoid it. The midwife saw Malina's mark when she was born and later traded the information for five potatoes and a cut of meat."

"That's horrible," Donna whispered. She threaded her arms through her bra. Dressing was an excuse not to look at him, and it busied her shaking hands.

"As is starvation," Fergus said. "Ya cannot blame a hungry peasant for needing food. That's what Elspeth said when we found out."

"It is horrible that the midwife had to be in that situation, but I don't think I'm as kind as Elspeth was. I can't see giving up a baby to murder." She pulled her long-sleeve shirt over her head and finally turned to face him.

Fergus looked as if he would reach for her, but he held back. He was still naked on the bed. A sheet draped over his waist, pulled down just enough to show his muscled hip.

"So what happened?"

"Knowing that the hunters would kill Malina if they found her, and then would investigate the entire MacGregor clan, Elspeth tried to get our niece out of the country."

Donna's hands shook. The pain in his voice was raw. She could picture running through a snowy forest with an infant in her arms. White puffs of breath and uneven ground. Trying to keep an infant warm. Scared. Cold.

"When warlocks marry, we give part of ourselves to our significant other so that they may develop some magick of their own, but it takes time. Elspeth was human. We were new to marriage, and my powers had not fully developed in her to protect her. I helped to distract some of the men looking for Malina so they could escape. When I finally caught up to them, it was too late. Elspeth had used up what little magick she possessed to bind Malina's cry and hide her from harm. When she wouldn't tell the witch hunter where she'd taken the child, he ran her through and left her for dead."

A tear slipped over Donna's cheek. "And she died in your arms, didn't she?"

"Aye. She did."

"And I'm guessing, since you have magick, you've been trying to bring her back ever since?"

Fergus nodded. "How did ya know that?"

"I can see it on your face. I can also see the pain and guilt." Donna tried to hide her sorrow. It felt as if her heart was breaking in half. What real claim did she have on this man? Despite the connection she felt, she realized they hadn't known each other long. There was no competing with ghosts. "I'm sorry she passed away, but this isn't cheating. If your wife loved you as much as you love her, then she wouldn't want you to feel guilty for this."

"Angus would agree with ya, but I'm not sure that's what my Elspeth would say. She was always a jealous one. She loved me very much." Fergus moved to sit on the edge of the bed. He folded his hands in his lap. "I haven't been with anyone else since her."

"Why me? Why now?"

"There is something about ya that draws me. I haven't felt this way since…" Fergus left the rest of his comment unspoken.

Donna took a deep breath. He couldn't even say it. "I'm not Elspeth. I'm rarely jealous of anything. I don't cook. I couldn't forgive the midwife for betraying a child. I don't always know the right thing to do or say, but I go with my gut." She walked around to his side of the bed. "I really like you, Gus. I like spending time with you. I would like to spend more time with you and see where this goes. But I'm only me. I will not replace a dead wife, and I will not compete with her ghost."

"I would not ask ya to."

"You might not say it, but that look on your face when you speak of her says more than your words ever could." Donna touched his face. "I want you. I want to stay here with you. I want to crawl into that bed and kiss you and pretend your past is not your past, and the pain in my chest right now is not real."

He placed his hand over hers and held her to him, and a very frightening realization came over her as she looked into his eyes. She loved him. Somehow, someway, she loved him. She knew it as sure as she knew the sun shone and birds sang. It just was. A natural, indisputable fact.

The pain became worse.

"Thank you for not lying to me," she whispered.

"Don't leave. Come back to bed. Stay. Please, Donna. I don't want ya to go."

"I, um…" She pulled her hand from his and scratched her forehead in distraction. "I have to go to work. I missed a shoot, and I have to make some calls, and I have an appointment."

The vague excuse was all she could come up with, even if everything she said was true.

"May I call on ya later?" Fergus grabbed her

camera off the floor and followed her as she made a move for the bedroom door. He handed it to her.

Donna nodded, unable to get any more words out as she left him. She hurried to the stairwell, not wanting to run into any of the family members on her way out the door. Luck was not with her.

Margareta stood in the front hall gazing up at the Christmas tree. She pointed at it, moving her finger to magickally rearrange a few ornaments, so they were no longer perfectly aligned. Seeing Donna, she chuckled. "Don't tell Cait. This will drive her to distraction."

Donna nodded and moved toward the front door.

"What it is it, dear?" Margareta followed her to the doorway.

"I'm late for work," Donna mumbled.

The woman looked worriedly up toward where Fergus's bedroom was and then back to Donna. She stared with a strange look on her face.

"Don't worry, I'm not going to tell anyone about anything." Donna glanced at the magickally decorated tree. "No one would believe me, and I value my reputation for sanity."

"Elspeth?" Margareta whispered.

"Yes. He told me about her." Donna

wondered at the dynamics of this family. Clearly they were close if generations of them had lived in the same house for presumably hundreds of years.

Margareta reached for her shoulder. Donna started to smile politely at the kind gesture when the woman suddenly pushed her aside and hurried out into the front yard. "Elspeth, wait!"

Donna gasped. She looked over the yard. The slender woman she'd had glimpses of around town a few times was walking toward the trees. Her brownish blonde hair flew behind her in the breeze and the hem of her green dress dragged in the snow behind her. There was a translucence to the woman's appearance that made her more of a projection or an apparition than an actual presence.

"Fergus!" Margareta ran to the doorway and screamed, "She's here. Elspeth is here."

Donna bit back her tears as she stumbled away from the house. She stared at the trees where the woman had disappeared until movement caught her attention.

"Elspeth?" Fergus appeared in the doorway fully dressed. "Are ya sure, Margareta? I do not see her."

Donna took small steps away from him, walking backward down the hill. Fergus found her and stiffened mid-motion. He glanced at

Margareta and then back to her, clearly torn as to which direction to run.

The cold caused the tears falling down her cheeks to sting. Donna shook her head in denial and lifted her hand to keep him from coming after her. She'd make the choice easy for him. She could not compete with the memory of Elspeth. There was no way she was competing with Elspeth now that she'd come back.

Chapter Nine

Fergus searched the woods for hours. He had not seen his wife, but Margareta had been so certain he had to keep looking. There were no tracks in the snow where his sister had claimed she'd appeared. That could only mean Elspeth was in spirit form, not corporeal. Spirits were hard to find, but not impossible. When searching proved fruitless, he then went to the stone altar in the back gardens and lit candles. He'd tried his spirit board many times. It had never worked. But now Elspeth was close. She'd been seen.

Had his feelings for Donna stirred his wife's spirit? Was it jealousy that had brought her back to him?

Donna.

Being with Donna had been like the answer to

a prophecy—meant to be. She was smart and witty, and a strange combination of sweet and saucy. Now, as he tried to call Elspeth to him, he felt as if he was betraying Donna. The guilt he'd felt over Elspeth was now amplified, as if he cheated on both women.

He needed to be here, calling Elspeth. Never had he been this close to finding her. He wanted to be with Donna, erasing that parting look of pain off her face. He'd never meant to hurt her. If he were honest with himself, he'd admit that he loved her.

He loved Donna.

He loved Elspeth.

The knowledge shamed him.

"Elspeth?" Fergus whispered, looking around the gardens bathed in moonlight and snow. "It feels like the night I lost ya, love, the cold snow and a bitter chill to the air. Do ya remember what I promised? Whatever lies ahead, I'll find you. I've tried, but I need your help, love. Ya were always the one who knew what I should do." He waited, but there was no answer. "Is this your way of saying ya approve of Donna? Do ya want me to move on?"

A strong gust of wind whipped over him, blowing out the candles and throwing the spirit board angrily into a shrub. The thick wood split in half on impact. Seconds later, the wind changed directions, ripping the shrub from the ground as it carried the broken board toward Fergus's head. He lifted his arms as the bush slammed into him. The impact knocked him over. The bush rolled down the cobblestone path toward the mansion.

Stunned, he lay on the ground, breathing hard. It would appear he had Elspeth's answer.

Chapter Ten

Donna huddled on her couch, staring at the display screen on the back of her camera. An angry, distorted face stared at her. She knew the woman was Elspeth by the long blonde-streaked brown hair and green dress. The ghostly image was locked in a scream.

What should have been naked Fergus on the sled had ended up being a series of strangely threatening photographs. Donna slowly flipped through them for the hundredth time. Fergus's face was blurred in the first one. Then there was the sheepdog she'd seen near Fergus laying in a grave partially covered in dirt. There was a squished insect on a window ledge. One picture depicted a cow with wide, frightened eyes. Another was an old mule. Yet another was a fallen butterfly. Then Donna as a child on the farm, crying and holding her bleeding head after she'd hit herself during a stick-fighting match with her imaginary friend. And finally the enraged Elspeth.

It didn't take a genius to interpret the message. Elspeth was warning Donna to stay away from Fergus or she'd kill her like an animal going to slaughter.

Donna pulled the knitted blanket close to her body. Thick, fuzzy pajama pants and slippers should have offered her plenty of warmth, but the room had been getting colder despite the furnace being on. She thought about running, but there was nowhere to go. She couldn't call Sheriff Johnson and tell him a ghost was threatening her. She didn't dare go back to the MacGregor mansion for fear that would make the spirit angrier.

The one thing she couldn't control was the pain she felt. She had fallen in love with Fergus. There was no hiding it, no denying it to herself. He cared for her. She'd seen it on his face when he'd watched her walk away. If she thought for a moment he could love her back, she'd fight Elspeth for him—scary, jealous supernatural witch and all.

Her lamplight began to flicker, and the temperature dropped dramatically as if Elspeth had heard the thought and come to answer the threat. The sound of wind whipped around the house, whistling loudly as it rattled the windows. A dog barked in warning.

"Oh, shit," Donna whispered. She hooked her camera strap over her neck, not for any other reason beyond muscle memory repeating an old habit. The barking outside grew louder only to be followed by a series of hard thuds coming from her ceiling. The lights flickered harder. Donna looked up, shaking with each paranormal bang. She held the blanket close and forced herself to stand. The front door was the closest escape. Footsteps began running down the hall toward her.

Donna crashed into her oversized photo display, knocking it over as she ran out of the house. Snow flurried all around her, reflecting enough moonlight so that she could see where she was going. There was only one destination that made sense—Fergus. Her slippers crunched through a hard sheet of ice covering the snow beneath. It gave her a little traction as she made her way to the MacGregor drive. She couldn't see the house yet, but that only made her run faster.

The dog barked again. She screamed at how close it sounded. When she frantically looked, nothing was there. Strange noises tormented her

—the soft ting of a cowbell, the cry of a donkey, the buzz of an invisible fly.

"Leave me alone, Elspeth," she cried, out of breath as she continued to run uphill. "You're dead. I'm not. I can be good for him."

Her answer came in the form of a rabid sheepdog. She screamed, dropping her knitted blanket as she ran harder. The beast forced her to turn toward the woods. She hurried for the shelter of the trees. Her heart pounded, drumming in her ears like a horse's hooves. She wasn't going to make it to Fergus. Elspeth was not going to let her.

The sound of her heart seemed to come from outside of herself until she realized it was the echo of the hooves.

"*Comhstach,*" a man's voice said. She recognized it as the same one that had been whispering in her house.

Donna could barely breathe. The horse stopped. Heavy boots landed on the ground and began to crush the snow, coming in her direction. If he walked directly past her inadequate hiding spot he'd surely discover her. She heard the long, sharp slide of metal. The invisible man had a sword.

Donna took the uncomfortable camera strap off her neck and tucked the equipment next to the tree beneath the brush. She crawled in the snow looking for better cover.

The footsteps found her. She turned, but no one was there, only impressions of boots crushing the snow as the ghost man came for her. She couldn't fight what wasn't there, but she knew he was angry and was going to kill her if she didn't give him what he wanted. Donna screamed. She pushed to her feet and ran while looking behind her for signs of evil in the moonlight.

Suddenly, a sharp object pierced her stomach. She turned forward, only to find she'd impaled herself on a low tree branch. Her breath caught, and she pulled away from the tree. Cradling her stomach, she stumbled and fell on the ground. The footprints stopped near her and for an instant she thought she saw a man's boots. She drew her head back sharply only to see the impression of a Medieval warrior stepping away from her with his bloodied sword as if he'd been the one who'd run her through. The man faded, and his voice echoed in his wake, "See if the devil will save ya and the babe now, *comhstach.*"

At first she felt nothing, just a confused sense of being hurt. Her eyes went to where she hid the camera as if suddenly protecting it was the most important thing in the world. Wait, no. Not a camera. A baby. She'd hidden a baby that couldn't cry. She had to protect the baby.

And then suddenly the pain came in a rush. She fell onto her side in the snow and gasped loudly as she clutched her stomach over the wound. Tears slid down her cheeks. She tried to speak, but only a moan came out.

"Elspeth? Where are ya? Where did ya go?"

She moaned louder at Fergus's voice.

"Donna?"

Donna lifted a bloodied hand as he appeared before her.

"Donna!" He kneeled beside her. His hands pressed over her wound as if he could stop it. "Oh, love, what did ya do? Not again. Not again. Oh, not again. Cait!"

"Gus," she said, desperate to get his frantic attention. There was so much she needed to tell him, but as he looked at her, his face changed. The gray faded from his temples. His hair grew as did his beard.

"Do not leave me," he begged, the voice strange as if it came from inside her mind.

She wanted to answer, but it hurt too badly. This was not how their story was supposed to end. She'd just found him.

"I'm coming with ya, my heart," Fergus said,

more like a plea. He began to look around the forest ground.

"Gus." Her voice broke whatever spell they were under and his hair returned to normal. Not knowing why she said it, she whispered, "Whatever is beyond, find me again."

"No! I will not lose ya, Donna." He gathered her in his arms and lifted. "Cait! Help me, Cait!"

Donna moaned in agony. Fergus's movements jolted her body as he carried her through the trees toward the mansion. She coughed, and her lips tasted of blood. The world began to dim and with darkness came blessed relief.

Chapter Eleven

Fergus continued to scream for his sister as he carried Donna from the woods. He'd followed Elspeth's spirit to where Donna lay. The wounds were too similar to be ignored. Elspeth in her green dress, run through with a sword. Donna in soggy stuffed rabbits on her feet and pink fuzzy pants, punctured in the exact same place by a tree.

"Cait!" he cried desperately. He couldn't lose her. Not now. Not like this. Not again. This was not how love was supposed to be. He was supposed to get forever.

He was powerless to save her. He didn't have the right kind of magick. But Cait did. She was a healer.

"Don't leave me, my heart," he begged. "Cait!"

"What is it?" Cait appeared on the front step as Fergus pushed past, taking Donna inside. The barrier of warmth greeted them as they came out of the cold into the perfect temperature of the house. He placed her on the floor. Cait instantly came beside him and placed her hands over Donna's wound.

"What happened?" Margareta demanded.

"We were supposed to have forever," he whispered.

Cait grabbed hold of Fergus's arm with one hand and began draining his power in order to fuel her own. Margareta placed her hand over Cait's, letting her take what she needed from her as well.

"Fergus, look," Margareta said.

He lifted his eyes from Donna to find Elspeth's spirit looking at him. His dead wife smiled, the same look he'd carried with him through the centuries.

"Elspeth?" He said her name in disbelief.

"Whatever lies ahead," Elspeth answered softly. She came forward and placed her hand over Cait's. Before Cait could stop it, Elspeth used the flow of power to drain her spirit into Donna.

Donna gasped and opened her eyes. Cait drew her hand back to reveal a healed stomach.

Fergus leaned over her, cupping her face. "Donna? Can ya hear me?"

She took several deep breaths. "Of course I can hear you. You're two inches away from my face."

He gave a small laugh of relief, happy she was alive. "Ya gave me a scare, lass. How are ya feeling?"

"Like…" Donna frowned. "Like I want to bake you cookies." She sighed heavily and mumbled, "Dammit, Elspeth. We don't bake in this lifetime."

"She gave herself to save ya," Fergus explained.

"No." Donna pushed up to a sitting position on the floor. "I remember everything. That part of my spirit has been trying to come back to me. Actually, all parts of my spirit have been trying to come back to me."

"That's why she was so comfortable with seeing magick," Cait said to Margareta as if the two of them had been discussing it and the mystery was now solved.

"All parts?" Fergus stroked Donna's hair away from her cheek. He felt his love in her. Elspeth, Donna, whatever she was called, he felt his soul being reflected back to him. This was his wife. Forever.

Donna smiled at Cait. "Thank you for healing me. I see your powers have gotten much stronger."

"I'm just glad I was nearby this time," Cait answered.

"Elspeth?" Margareta reached to hug her. "I'm so happy to see ya. I have waited a long time to thank ya for saving my daughter."

"Donna," Donna corrected, returning the hug of her old friend. "Elspeth was a past life, but you're welcome. Part of me can't believe how grown Malina is. I'm so glad she's all right. The other part of me can't believe I was ever in a fight with a witch hunter."

"We never told Malina ya died saving her," Margareta said. "Perhaps we should have, but after Fergus finally delivered her to England, we didn't see her for a very long time. When she came back to us, she said she felt like an outsider, no matter how much we told her we loved her. She knew how much we all missed Elspeth, and that ya died in the witch trials. It never seemed right to let her carry that blame. But she knows all about ya."

"Of course." Donna nodded. "You shouldn't put that kind of guilt on a kid. What happened was not Malina's fault."

"Donna, I don't understand. Ya said parts?" Fergus pulled her away from Margareta so that he could hold her. "What did ya mean when ya said all parts of your spirit came back?"

"You, my dear, have not gotten better with your spells," Donna whispered, cupping his face in her hands. "And my abilities in the kitchen were a victim of their side effects. At least that's the excuse I'm going to tell the rest of your family."

"I tried. I'm so sorry. I tried everything to bring ya back sooner." Fergus was afraid to let go, to stop looking at her face. He wanted to hold her, make love to her, and stare at her so she couldn't disappear from his life again.

"Oh, I can remember that too. You brought me back plenty of times, husband. You brought me back as a fly and then squished me. You brought me back as a sheepdog and then named me Martin! You made me sleep on the floor."

"Oh, Fergus," Margareta scolded. "Ya didn't."

"Martin?" Cait laughed. "Ya cursed that dog for a century for chewing your favorite boots."

"Hey, that's right," Fergus said. "Ya ate my boots."

"They were ugly," Donna stated. "It was the only way to get you to stop wearing them."

"Well, ya say I squished ya? Let's just call it

even. I forgive ya for the boots." He couldn't keep the grin off his face. Four hundred years had culminated into this perfect moment. He may never stop smiling again.

"Even? Oh, hardly, I'm just getting started. We have four hundred years of reincarnations to discuss, Mr. MacGregor. There's the cow and the—"

Fergus kissed her to quiet her. Then he pulled her to her feet as he stood, not letting go. He lifted her into his arms and carried her up the stairs. "It looks as if I did all right this last time."

"Hey, Margareta, do these tree ornaments look off to ya?" Cait asked behind them.

"I don't know what you're talking about," Margareta answered.

Fergus walked faster, wanting to get Donna alone. Making love to her once had not been enough.

"You think you did all right? My past life tried to kill me in this life, twice, in an effort to make me remember her." Donna tapped her finger against the tip of his nose before lightly pinching the tip and wiggling it.

"Twice?" He continued up the stairs and onto the landing.

"The first time was when I was a kid. She hit me with a stick. I think she was trying to knock some sense into me, or something. I don't know. It seems a bunch of little accidents and oddities in my life can be attributed to Elspeth trying to communicate."

"Ya can't blame me for that. Technically ya hit yourself." He tried to kiss her, but she pulled back.

"Fine. Past-me hit present-me with a stick. I'm Elspeth, but not Elspeth. However, I guess we're kind of even on this point since she did try to kill you too."

"Oh?" He paused in his pursuit of her mouth.

"The enchanted cookie baking." Donna laughed. "I can guarantee the happy homemaker neighbor deliveries were not this lifetime's idea." Suddenly, her laughter stopped. "That's not going to happen anymore, is it? I mean, I'll be arrested for poisoning someone if I keep that up."

"Well, I do need ya to make me at least one more batch." Fergus lifted his hand, throwing open the bedroom door without touching it.

She arched a brow. He had to be joking.

"I've already called a MacGregor challenge as soon as Euann is back from New York. He, Rory, and Malina will have to eat an entire pan of whatever ya bake as punishment for their joke gone wrong. They should have never given ya that gift basket. It was meant in jest for me to find, but I didn't find it, and they do not know ya well enough to pull such pranks."

"Actually, it is kind of funny," Donna admitted. "I was so flustered by you and thought I was losing my sanity because of all the baking enchantment type episodes, that I yelled at you when I should have just laughed and accepted the joke for what it was. I'm sorry I yelled at you. You're not a jerk. I should have apologized to you before now about that."

"I'll let ya make it up to me now." Fergus grinned wickedly. He made their clothes melt from their bodies as he carried her to the bed. All the guilt was gone. The years no longer mattered. He had his heart back. Donna. His wife.

He laid her on the bed and then motioned his hand, slamming the door shut to give them privacy. His lips pressed to hers, kissing her deeply. He let her feel all the love he had for her. Everything he was belonged to her. It always had.

Pulling back, he grinned. "Ya know, I remember being rather fond of a mule."

"We are never to mention my being a mule again." Donna's tone was stern.

"Oh, but love, ya were such a fine ass. I did enjoy riding ya." He reached around to grab a firm butt cheek.

"Shut up and make love to me already."

Donna pushed him onto his back and took control. Soon their bodies were joining in a fevered rhythm as if trying to make up for lost time. As they met with a shaky climax, she whispered, "*Gráim thú.*"

"Aye, Donna, I love ya too."

Chapter Twelve

EPILOGUE

Green Vallis Annual Winter Skate

Over a thousand sparkling holiday lights arched over the stretch of frozen creek to welcome the townsfolk as they skated through MacGregor land. Donna had been wrong. Her new-old family didn't think they were better than the townsfolk. They simply needed to protect their magick from prying eyes. After remembering her own experience at the hands of the witch hunters, she could appreciate their need to keep mortals unaware.

Donna lifted her new camera as another couple skated across the end of the course. Unfortunately, when she'd had her little entranced episode in the forest, her instinct had been to hide the camera like it was Malina. The camera did not survive the puddle she'd mindlessly shoved it in.

The skating couple smiled at her and waved up to where she stood on a platform. Considering how rich her family was, she didn't need to worry about money. And yet she felt some thrill in knowing this year she'd be selling a lot of skate pictures, thanks to the lovely set up.

The creek decorations had been carefully planned by Cait. They were a perfect progression of colors from white to blue to green to red and then white again. At the end hung giant lighted snowflakes.

Fergus wrapped his arms around her from behind. The unmistakable press of his interest molded against her hip as he leaned into her. "I think ya took enough. Let's go sneak away to bed."

"After everyone is done skating," Donna answered, taking another shot.

"We can't after," Fergus grumbled. He kissed her neck, sending tiny shivers of desire over her. She knew instantly he was trying to use his magick to heighten her physical desire for him. It was working. The sensation shot straight down to settle between her legs.

"And why is that?" she whispered, turning in his embrace.

"MacGregor challenge." He grinned like a mischievous child. "We're going to skate the course naked."

"You know, I should probably worry about how much you all seem to enjoy being naked." Donna let her hand skim down to cup his ass. "It's a good thing you look so wonderful doing it."

"Hey, did you get us?" an irritated woman shouted.

Donna blinked, letting go of Fergus's ass as she turned back to the creek. Grumpy Mrs. Callister stood on the ice with her thirty-some-thing daughter, Grace.

Automatically, she lifted her camera.

"Aye," Fergus answered before Donna could take the picture. "And it was a lovely vision, lassie."

Mrs. Callister simpered and smiled at the compliment. The two ladies skated off before Donna could take the shot.

"You're lucky I lost the Elspeth jealous streak," Donna said.

"I'm lucky because I found ya twice." Fergus lifted her hand and slid a gold band onto her finger. "I know we technically did this already a lifetime ago, but what do ya say? Marry me again, my heart, in this lifetime?"

"Yes, Gus." Donna sniffed back happy tears.

"I'll marry you in this life, and the next, and the next and the…wait. Can I take that back? You'd better not be giving me any other lifetimes. I like this one. If anything happens to me, with your spell casting, you'll end up keeping your promise by getting married to a donkey."

"Quiet your tongue." He kissed her to silence her teasing. Skating townsfolk began to cheer loudly below them. Donna laughed against his mouth but had no intention of stopping what they were doing. Ever.

The End

The Series Continues...

WARLOCKS MACGREGOR®® 4: CAULDRONS AND CONFESSIONS

Malina MacGregor is more than just a delicate flower in need of manly protection, but you wouldn't know if by the slew of male family members who show up anytime she tries to go on a date. Sure, she's made some poor choices in men in the past—like the demon she mistakenly hooked up with in Las Vegas years ago. But that was then, and this is now, and she more than made up for that mistake.

Darragh "Dar" Lahey may be a luck demon, but his luck ran out the night he met the temptress—Malina. Now he's back, and he has an axe to grind. Malina needs to pay for what she did to him, and the supernatural attacks he's firing at her magickal family is just the beginning. There is only one hitch in his plans for revenge—even after all this time the stubborn woman can still make his heart ache, and his body burn with need.

Warning: Contains yummy, hot, mischievous MacGregors who are almost certainly up to no good on their quest to find true love.

For more information, visit www.
MichellePillow.com

Warlocks MacGregor® 4: Cauldrons and Confessions Extended Excerpt

Nevada Desert, 1960

"How did you find me?" Malina couldn't meet her brother's gaze, but she felt Niall staring at her in disappointment from across the car as he drove her further and further away from Las Vegas. Eventually, the bright lights of the city faded in the rearview mirrors to an insignificant spot on the horizon. On any other night, the view might have been beautiful.

"Do ya really think you're hard to track?" Niall gave a sarcastic laugh that held no humor. His Scottish accent was a stark contrast to her softer English one.

Malina tapped her fingers against the soda bottle on her lap not drinking it. Her eyes focused on the hem of his kilt. For once his clothes had blended in. When he came for her at the hotel, people assumed he was a performer, not the evil-hunting warlock he actually was. If there was an evil threat to be dealt with, there was no better man than Niall.

"The family always knows where ya are," he continued. "Da sent me to bring ya home. Mobsters and degenerates are not the company for a lady to keep. I must say I'm disappointed in ya, Malina. A warlock of your abilities and ya squander it on booze and losers. Sometimes I think ma made a mistake sending ya away from the clan during the witch trials. Ya were a baby, so in some ways, it was not your fault that ya don't fully understand the concept of family loyalty and duty. However, at over three hundred years old ya should know better."

His words stung, but she had no defense. It's not like she needed to be reminded that she was an outsider because of some humans in East Lothian, Scotland decided witches needed to be burned at the stake when she was born. One look at the birthmark on her ass and they would have declared her the child of Satan. Their beloved Aunt Elspeth had sacrificed herself so that Malina could live. The family liked to remind her of that fact as well.

"When are you going to give up these silly rebellions? I think ya get some sick pleasure in making us rescue ya. Is that it?" he demanded. "How many more will there be, Malina? How many bad decisions and stupid mistakes? Lord Barrison, the rogue—"

"That was the seventeen hundreds," she protested.

"My point exactly. Barrison was trying to get ya to Gretna Green to elope for our family money. The cardsharp in London whose name we could never fully ascertain. George, the horse thief. Billy, the cattle rustler. Jack, the moonshiner. Your life has been a repeat of the same bad judgments. And now ya have graduated to mass murderers." Niall jerked the car roughly to the right to avoid a cactus.

Malina slid on the seat and had to grab the door to right herself. The dots of blood on her hand reminded her of the casino shooting she'd just witnessed. The blood stained her fancy dress. Malina began picking at her hand to scrape it off. The agony was almost too much. "I didn't know he…" She couldn't say the words.

When Niall first came to her to tell her the man she was with was a demon, she hadn't wanted to believe him. She'd demanded proof. It was because of her all those people had been hurt and probably killed. If she had let Niall stop the demon sooner, those innocent people would have been safe.

"That's my point. Ya never know, and ya never think. Each and every time ya have called me to help ya, and each time ya didn't know he was a bad guy. Tell me, how could ya not know that the man ya were with is a demon?" Niall took a deep breath. "Drink it."

"His name is Dar," she said, not liking the word demon.

"Drink it," he repeated.

"I don't want to," Malina denied. Just hours before she had been so happy. Now the pain was unbearable. This was much worse than the time she'd ben duped by a gold digging rogue. Barrison had wanted her money. Dar wanted her family's magick. Oh, and he had done such a great job making her fall for him so that the betrayal of who he was combined with the ache of loss in her chest. It had all been a lie—every single second.

The headlights revealed the long stretch of endless desert, a wasteland of cacti and sand. After they had passed a rundown service station, the road disappeared, and the ride became bumpy.

A tear slipped down her cheek. "What are you going to do, Niall?"

"Ya know what I have to do," Niall answered. "Now drink it. We're almost there. I don't want the demon taking possession of ya. I would not be able to live with myself if I was forced to subdue ya."

"Maybe we're wrong," she said, though the logic of what she'd seen contradicted her vain hope. "Maybe he can explain himself."

"He's a demon," Niall stated as if that was all the proof he needed. "What other proof do ya need? If my word is not good enough, then ya saw what he did."

He stopped the car a little too quickly, and she was thrust toward the dash. She gripped the soda bottle as liquid splashed over the top.

He was right. She'd messed up this time, worse than ever before. She was a poor excuse for a warlock. All this time she acted like she had some-thing to prove, that she was just as good as all her brothers, and cousins, and the entire MacGregor clan, and really she was the outcast screw up. She didn't even know a demon when it pinched her on the witch's mark.

"Trust your family," Niall insisted. "Family is the only thing ya can count on in this life, my sister."

Malina chugged the warm liquid laced with magical herbs. The numbness took effect almost instantly, and she felt herself calming and becoming more compliant. Mumbling as if she was suddenly under the influence of an entire bottle of tequila, she said, "Niall, this doesn't feel like a protection spell. I feel... strange."

"It's for your own good. That will make this easier. I promise I'll keep my word. None of the other's will ever know what ya did. Trust me. We'll clean up this mess and then it will be like it never happened. I'll take care of ya. I will always take care of ya," Niall said, taking the empty bottle from her. "Now, get out of the car. We have a demon to kill."

Malina blinked a few times before obeying. Everything became a white fog as she met Niall by the trunk of the car. Her limbs hung heavy at her sides. Her eyes became fixated on the trunk as it opened. Dark eyes met hers. Those eyes didn't reflect evil. They appeared frightened, and a little angry. Dar didn't look like a demon. He looked like a man—a man tied up in the back of a car in the middle of the desert at night. Maybe they were wrong. Maybe this didn't have to be done.

A gag pulled tight to Dar's handsome mouth, muffling his words as he tried to speak. Malina couldn't be sure if it were a plea or a curse.

"It's as we discussed back at the hotel. He'll try to trick you. The evil ones always do. You must not believe their lies." Niall drew a sharp knife from his waist. The carved steel gleamed as Niall's magick swirled up from his hand. He reached for Dar, using magick to strengthen his grip as he pulled the man from the trunk and began dragging him around to the front of the vehicle.

Niall pointed the blade at the ground and began to chant under his breath. Sand swirled over the desert as it lifted up and flew into the sky to create a grave.

"Wait." Malina tried to bring up her powers, but they were slow to come to her. "Are you sure? He looks human."

Niall didn't wait, didn't listen as if he knew she'd lose her nerve. He thrust the demon blade into Dar. The man's once handsome face morphed into a hideous beast, giving her the last shred of evidence she needed. Kind eyes darkened into black pits as horns grew from his head. She screamed, backing up so quickly she tripped over the car. Niall didn't miss a beat. He threw the demon into the hole and lifted his hand to create fire. Within seconds, Dar was burning, and the smell of his death was wafting over her numbed senses.

Confusion and pain filled her, combining with embarrassment. Niall was right. She'd fucked up yet again. She pushed to her feet and stumbled to the graveside. The smell was overwhelming, and she gagged. "I don't feel well." The red fire in the pit roared angrily as she looked down into it. She wanted to jump in and die too. "I feel dizzy."

Tonight, life as she knew it had ended. There was no coming back from the feeling of loss she felt. Blackness came for her, and she didn't fight it. She didn't care if she never woke up again.

Warlocks MacGregor® Series

Love Potions

Spellbound

Stirring Up Trouble

Cauldrons and Confessions

Spirits and Spells

Kisses and Curses

Magick and Mischief

A Dash of Destiny

More Coming Soon

Visit www.MichellePillow.com for details.

About Michelle M. Pillow

***New York Times* & *USA TODAY*
Bestselling Author**

Michelle loves to travel and try new things, whether it's a paranormal investigation of an old Vaudeville Theatre or climbing Mayan temples in Belize. She believes life is an adventure fueled by copious amounts of coffee.

Newly relocated to the American South, Michelle is involved in various film and documentary projects with her talented director husband. She is mom to a fantastic artist. And she's managed by a dog and cat who make sure she's meeting her deadlines.

For the most part she can be found wearing pajama pants and working in her office. There may or may not be dancing. It's all part of the creative process.

Come say hello! Michelle loves talking with readers on social media!

www.MichellePillow.com

facebook.com/AuthorMichellePillow

twitter.com/michellepillow

instagram.com/michellempillow

bookbub.com/authors/michelle-m-pillow

goodreads.com/Michelle_Pillow

amazon.com/author/michellepillow

youtube.com/michellepillow

pinterest.com/michellepillow

Newsletter

To stay informed about when a new book in the series installments is released, sign up for updates:

Sign up for Michelle's Newsletter

michellepillow.com/author-updates

Complimentary Material

CHECK IT OUT BEFORE YOU BUY!

Rebellious Prince
Captured by a Dragon-Shifter
A Modern Day Dragon Lords World Story

Cat-shifter Prince Rafe knows that technically he's supposed to be going to Earth to find a bride, but he doesn't see the need to rush things. While his dragon-shifter neighbors appear all too eager to claim their mates and settle down, he's all for putting that final moment off and enjoying his little trips through the portal. Yeah, yeah, eventually he'll have to marry and set a good example for his people because on his planet females are rare and they need to have children and blah blah blah. But honestly, cat-shifters are known to embrace their feral side and it would take a very impressive female to tame his.

Then he sees Jenna Kearney and all bets are off.

**To find out more about Michelle's books
visit www.MichellePillow.com**

Please Leave a Review

THANK YOU FOR READING!

Please take a moment to share your thoughts by reviewing this book.

Be sure to check out Michelle's other titles at
www.MichellePillow.com